This book belongs to

....

Ten Little Pumpkins

Written by Rosie Greening • Illustrated by Lara Ede

make
believe
ideas

10 little pumpkins
are growing in a line.

Then a **farmer** picks one up and that **leaves** . . .

9 little pumpkins
bouncing in a crate.

One decides to **bounce away**
and that leaves . . .

8 little pumpkins
in a bumpy hayride heaven.

A pony **carries** one away
and that leaves . . .

Then one pumpkin disappears
and that leaves . . .

POOF!

One jumps out to trick-or-treat and that leaves . . .

5 little pumpkins grinning in the store.

Delicious vegetables

Pumpkins for sale

4 little pumpkins
as happy as can be.

Then a **spooky ghost** grabs one
and that **leaves** . . . .

Boo!

Yummy tomatoes

3 little pumpkins playing **peekaboo.**

Buy two, get one free

Basket bundle

2 little pumpkins having lots of fun.

Bargain cauliflower

10 little pumpkins make such a **perfect** scene,

glowing all together on
the night of Halloween!